Life is a song, so sing along
Follow the path of your heart.

— Emma Rosenau

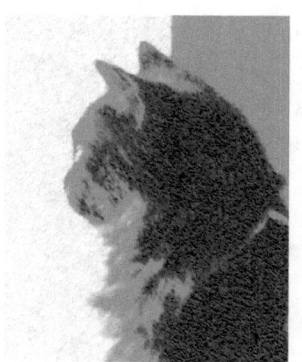

Milo

Milo

By Sharon Waters

When I headed for college, I took a goldfish along. My little fish buddy spent the summers swimming in our back porch rain barrel, and each fall I'd retrieve him to make our journey back to college. I could disregard the people who questioned my efforts on behalf of a goldfish; I needed some creature for company. After college I followed the traditional path to suburbia, marriage, and kids. But by the time my first marriage was falling apart I had also accumulated a petting zoo in my back yard. I had six peacocks, thirty ducks, nine rabbits, dozens of chickens, and two goats. They all got along well as they wandered around the yard, and the school bus driver would stop outside my house each morning so the kids could begin their day with a few minutes look at my peaceable kingdom.

The animals filled up my yard, the inside of my house, and whatever I felt was missing for me. I hatched chickens and baby peacocks in an incubator in my dining room while six cockatiels, also in the dining room, were constantly laying eggs and hatching more cockatiels all on their own. Occasionally the laying hens got through the back door and dashed inside to find their place in the dining room hatchery until I put them out again. The last of the feathered friends to join my household was Pippinella, a juvenile yellow naped Amazon parrot. She was bright, funny, and I loved her to death. After sharing thirty years together — and Pippy was expected to live to one hundred — she died from chewing on a toy that contained lead. The bottom fell out of my life; my negligence had been a factor in my best friend's death.

After my divorce I eventually had to move, and that put a check on what was beginning to look like an animal hoarding situation. Reluctantly, I sold a few animals and found suitable farm homes for most of the rest. My three children, who had been such a focus for me, grew up and went off to college and their own lives; I was moving beyond my half acre suburban home and 'married with family' life. I sold my house and moved to a condo in Boston, taking just three cats and Pippy, who was still with me at that time. I missed my petting zoo menagerie except perhaps for the goats, whose days were numbered anyway since they had been eating the siding on my house. I became a busy working city girl with a high tech job and graduate school classes. I had little time or space for more than the cats and Pippy in my urban apartment. But then it turned 2001. High tech departments that I worked in were taking a beating, tech jobs were vanishing, and I left Boston for the less expensive north shore and the quiet of the seaside. With less work and more time, I added two dogs, a cat named Billie, and Milo.

Cat Milo had a quirky imagination and would dash madly about a room, boxing phantom opponents at every turn. He liked to be chased, and it was clear he was conjuring you up to be a sneak attacker, that with his exceptional speed and cunning he could outrun and outwit. With Milo, everything required an excessive reaction. The first time he saw the flutter of snowflakes through an open door, Milo went off like popcorn. He landed hanging onto a door jamb just below the ceiling. His expression reflected his antics, and he gave new meaning to the term "wild eyed."

Not everything Milo did amused me, but it amused Milo. He had the biggest canine teeth I've ever seen on a cat, and he liked to use them. Once he went through an entire case of fifty small cardboard boxes I had ordered for a craft project, biting a single neat hole in every box, just enough to ruin every one of them. He enjoyed the thrill of mass destruction. I got used to it, and for years I never sent out a letter that didn't have Milo's signature tooth puncture mark in the corner of the paper. Milo was destructive, but the entertainment and companionship he added to my little household made up for it.

After a lifetime of managing a full-sized house and yard or apartments with the parade of pets, I sold it all and moved into an RV. The extreme downsizing left me with just some essential household items and my three remaining animals — the dogs Cricket and Magic, and Milo. I worried how Milo would adjust, but to my amazement, he was the least fazed by the transition. He slept during the days of travel, but was up to his usual mischief at night. We were in tight quarters so Milo decided he was one of the dogs. He slept with us and spent enough time head butting and licking the dogs that they accepted him as one of the pack.

Then it was really time to hit the road. It was freezing when we left New England to seek warmer weather in the South, but we departed in early January anyway. It never warmed up and we fought the intense cold the whole way to Florida. Everything was a problem except my trusty diesel engine, the dogs, and Milo. I could depend on them; the animals forgave me a difficult trip and we made the best of everything as long as we were together. On nights too cold to spend more than a few minutes outside, I'd load the dogs into a shopping cart and walk them through whichever Walmart was providing us a place to park that night. We purchased little, but wandered along the aisles just to spend time in the warmth of the store. Milo grew a thicker coat of fur, and spent more time huddling with us at night.

That winter we went over five thousand miles from Massachusetts, to Florida, and back to Massachusetts. The whole adventure was a triumph — the transition to life in the RV, the epic journey, the particular bonding with my pets. But after we'd been back home for a few months, one day Milo went missing and my whole world turned upside down. I had come home later than usual on a warm evening, and either he slipped out the door I had opened in the dark, or perhaps I had left a window open far enough for him to go through. Milo was missing, and like my failure to protect Pippy, it was my fault.

This was so unthinkable that at first I froze. What got me moving was a phone call from a neighbor just a few blocks away. That morning she had found Milo's harness with my phone number on the tag in the bushes near her house. I was relieved to feel Milo was still in the neighborhood, but distressed he had separated himself from his harness with ID tag. How would anyone even know he was lost if he was missing the ID that linked him to me? I printed up two hundred flyers, and went on a mission to make the best of every one of them. Every tree, every telephone pole got a Missing Cat flyer. I knocked on doors, rang doorbells, and talked to neighborhood people directly while putting a flyer in their hands. Even if they hadn't seen him, they would know how much I cared, and we would all keep looking.

I felt the absence of Milo throughout the daily routine, the morning animal feeding, the checks during the day to make sure each animal was accounted for. I'd find myself looking in the hat basket on the top bunk, which was his favorite napping spot. Surely he was sleeping in there as usual, but he wouldn't be. I'd leash up the dogs again and do another tour of the neighborhood.

The only place that wasn't blanketed with flyers was a wooded area which overlooked the neighborhood. It was a step back in time, with the foundation of a small Revolutionary War earthen works fort at one end. Covered with scrub trees and riddled with hillocks, it was a hiding place for everything that wanted access to the street without being seen. I had walked the dogs there frequently before the coyotes that harassed the neighborhood pets moved in. I had avoided it this summer, but now felt compelled to visit it again in the quest for Milo.

A few homeless men sheltered there during the warmer months, and I wasn't surprised to see evidence of them near the old fort. Their tents and the surrounding flotsam discarded by those better off than these men showed through the undergrowth that had overtaken the small paths this summer.

"Hello," I said. "Have you seen a fluffy black cat up here?"

"Yes'm, I have, just twenty minutes ago. Ran after 'im but didn't catch 'im, though."

"Did he look like this picture on the flyer?"

"Sure did, exactly. Really fluffy tail, right?"

"Yes. Well, if you catch him, there is a reward. Would you let anyone else up here know too, please?"

"Reward?...surely."

And the dogs and I were off through the undergrowth, me calling for Milo and hoping the dogs would pick up the scent of their friend. But nothing came of our search, or the conversation with the homeless man.

The frantic search for Milo became a lingering angst over the next few weeks. I'd stop by the neighbors who were keeping an eye out for him, but we'd end up talking about the possibility of Milo encountering a coyote, and I'd want to move my thoughts to something else. I said things like "Well, at least it must be over." Or "He was such a friendly cat, he's probably found a new home with someone that takes good care of him." But I felt no better at all. I thought of Milo alone, hungry, scared. It made for restless nights.

Several weeks later I was preparing for a trip to attend a music festival. There was a 'no dogs' policy at the festival, so I planned to leave the dogs with family along the way. I had anticipated all winter that without the dogs, it would be the ultimate bonding trip for Milo and me. For months I had looked forward to just the two of us sharing the road and a week at the festival. Milo would be the attraction for the kids, someone to play with and to entertain — all you needed was Milo and a string. At night he'd be my animal buddy. But now he was missing; I'd be without an animal companion for the first time since I could remember, and Milo would never have his special trip.

I tried intellectualizing the relative insignificance of a mere cat, but it wasn't working, and on the way to the festival, it got crazy. It was a long trip and on the second day of driving I decided to take the even longer route. My thoughts were on overdrive and I decided it more likely that I would pass a pet store if I got off the interstate. And what would I do if I did pass a pet store? Get another cat? Spend the day looking at kittens? I was missing Milo and obviously had spent too many hours with myself while on the road. It was just as well I didn't complicate things by getting another cat on the way, and after ten long hours of driving I finally pulled into the festival grounds. It had been raining there for days. I was directed to designated RV parking, where my RV immediately sank half way up its hubcaps in the mud. It was late in a long day for everyone, and I was soon deserted to contemplate my situation. I was feeling as low to the ground as my RV.

Help came to assist with the RV the next morning. A truck hauled it out of the mud and I resigned myself to making the best of this trip. It turned cold and rainy, but I was among exceptionally friendly and gracious people. I did my best to join in the festival and put on a good face for those who had invited me to come again this year. It was like a piece of Woodstock without the drugs for those who remembered, and a small version of it for those too young to remember. Dress was personal and creative — a blend of hippie, Renaissance, gypsy, and the middle east. I dug out my festival wear but watched from the sidelines.

My neighbors at RV parking were kind and caring free spirits. One who called himself Seeker was directly across from me and we quickly made acquaintance. Seeker dressed in layers of fringed leather and a wide brimmed hat with a lot of feathers. He was somewhere beyond middle aged, had shoulder length hair with a receding hairline, and seemed to have been waiting for an epiphany that never came in his life. Like many others at the festival he had been employed in a mainstream job for much of his life, but had been looking for a way to leave it. He confided that he had recently bought an ice cream truck to supplement a fixed income, but that the refrigeration generator didn't work and ice to keep the ice cream bars solid would only last three hours.

I spent much of the time just hanging out with Seeker and a few others. The festival celebrated community and was intended to encourage the artistic spirit, especially when it came to music. One afternoon we listened to the festival radio station, and the conversation was about Appalachia and the sad songs that were born in that hard place. But when it came to enthusiasm, the drummers were the hit of the festival. They played day and night until their incessant drumming was the heartbeat of us all.

I was feeling better, but the grief over missing Milo followed me around like a shadow. I wondered if I should even have come without him, but what would people think? That I was so upset over a cat that I stayed home? Would someone be insensitive about the extent of my distress over a cat? Toward the end of the festival I had another call from the neighbor back home who had found Milo's harness. She had been putting out food, canned tuna, for Milo every night in hopes he'd show up. She was sure she'd catch him, but it became wishful thinking, and I waited for the call that he'd been caught — but that call didn't come.

Then the festival was over and I packed up for my trip home. There was another long drive and I picked up the dogs along the way. Hours of traveling left me time to run through all the possible fates of Milo. Milo would just show up outside the RV when we got back. Someone had caught him and he was at their house. He was in a shelter somewhere. But mostly I began to think I should get adjusted to being without him.

When I got home, I had barely turned the engine off when I was told there was a message about Milo. The neighbor who had been feeding him discovered he was living only one house away; he had been seen coming and going from a small hole under a porch only a few houses from where he had first lost his harness. Apparently he had taken up living under the porch and emerged in the evening to look for the tuna left by my concerned neighbor. I hadn't been home ten minutes when I was on my way over to see if Milo could be found. I called "Milo, Milo" through the hole under the porch until I heard a little mewing that seemed so far away under the house. I kept calling and Milo came closer from under the house, to under the porch, until his familiar nose was sticking out of the hole. He looked bedraggled with dirty, matted fur. He was skittish and came close to me, but not enough so I could get my hands around him. If I grabbed for him, would he retreat out of reach? I forgot to breathe as I ran home, opened a can of tuna, and ran back.

Milo was still in his hideout, and the tuna worked to bring my starving friend close enough that I could grab him. It was two blocks to get him back to the RV — so close, would I make it back without losing hold of him? I found the balance between holding on tight and not crushing him to death. When I closed the RV door behind us, Milo wobbled around while the dogs and I and Milo adjusted to the idea that he was back home again. My thoughts were numb, and then the grief I'd had of missing Milo went into euphoric reverse.

A week later we were settling in to the idea that Milo had returned to us. He looked less bewildered, gained weight, and rediscovered his hiding place in the hat basket. The two dogs reverted to a threesome with Milo and bedtime was back to our relaxed routine. There was another warm spell. It was a lazy afternoon and the RV interior was heating up. I opened the windows and went into the back bedroom to read a book. It was noonday quiet except for the faint call of seagulls down by the beach, and I was appreciating the light breeze. But when I looked up from my book, there was Milo going out the opened window. I don't remember the dash to grab him, just that I got to him before he disappeared completely out the opening. So that's how he had gotten out… I closed the window and have not opened it again since.

Notes